P9-DHP-550

THE BINDER OF DOOM

SPEEDAH-CHEETAH

by Troy Cummings

BRANCHES™
SCHOLASTIC INC.

READ MORE BOOKS IN THE BINDER OF DOOM SERIES!

1 

2 

3 

4 

HAVE YOU READ ALL OF THE NOTEBOOK OF DOOM BOOKS?

1 

2 

3 

4 

5 

6 

7 

8 

9 

10 

11 

12 

13 

COLLECT THEM ALL!

SCHOLASTIC.COM/DOOM

TABLE OF CONTENTS

To Michael and Lee: Thanks for drawing monsters with me!

Library of Congress Cataloging-in-Publication Data

Names: Cummings, Troy, author. | Cummings, Troy. Binder of doom ; 3.

Title: Speedah-cheetah / Troy Cummings.

Description: First edition. | New York : Branches/Scholastic Inc., 2020. | Series: Binder of Doom ; 3 | Audience: Ages 6-8. | Audience: K to Grade 3. |

Summary: It is time for the Stermont Derby, a race around downtown Stermont in homemade vehicles, and Alexander, Nikki, and Rip are planning to compete, but so is a new monster, a Speedah-cheetah - and in addition to a diet of rotten eggs it plans on eating the race losers, especially the members of the Super Secret Monster Patrol.

Identifiers: LCCN 2019025340 | ISBN 9781338314724 (paperback) | ISBN 9781338314731 (library binding)

Subjects: LCSH: Monsters - Juvenile fiction. | Soap box derbies - Juvenile fiction. | Best friends - Juvenile fiction. | Horror tales. | CYAC: Monsters - Fiction. | Soap box derbies - Fiction. | Best friends - Fiction. | Friendship - Fiction. | Horror stories. | LCGFT: Horror fiction.

Classification: LCC PZ7.C91494 Sp 2020 | DDC 813.6 [Fic] - dc2 LC record available at https://lccn.loc.gov/2019025340

10 9 8 7 6 5 4 3 2 1 20 21 22 23 24

Printed in China 62

First edition, February 2020

Edited by Katie Carella

Book design by Troy Cummings and Sarah Dvojack

FAST TRACK

VROOOOM!

Alexander gripped the controls as his race car shot around the track, hugging the curves and making impossible jumps.

He was in the garage, racing his friends Rip and Nikki on his dad's old electric race track.

"See ya, slowpokes!" shouted Rip as his car pulled ahead.

"No way!" said Alexander. He hit the gas.

"Watch out for the curve!" warned Nikki.

SMACK! Alexander's car crashed into Rip's. Their cars flew off the track as Nikki's zipped across the finish line.

Alexander's dad cheered, "Nikki wins!"

He handed Nikki a first-place medal.

Then he leaned in to speak to Alexander and Rip. "You two are going to have to drive smarter if you want to win the big race this weekend."

"What race?" asked Alexander.

"The Stermont Derby!" said Alexander's dad. He pointed to a poster on the wall.

STERMONT DERBY
Race around downtown Stermont in homemade vehicles!
ANYTHING ON WHEELS!
FIRST PRIZE
$500!
SECOND PRIZE
COUPON FOR 10% OFF CARPET CLEANING!
THIRD PRIZE
NOTHING!
START
FINISH
TOWN SQUARE
DERWOOD PARK
SPONSORED BY STERMONT REALTY

"Whoa!" said Rip. "The winner gets five hundred bucks!"

"Plus, we get to make our own cars!" said Nikki.

"Yeah! You'll be designing your race cars at maker-camp tomorrow. But now I'm afraid Rip and Nikki need to race home for dinner," said Alexander's dad. "Al, you can do a couple more laps while I put on some chili."

"Okay, Dad," said Alexander as his dad headed inside. Then he whispered to his friends. "I'll see you tomorrow morning for you-know-what. We'll meet at our top-secret you-know-where before camp."

Rip and Nikki winked at Alexander as they left.

The three of them were members of a club called the Super Secret Monster Patrol. The S.S.M.P. protected Stermont from monsters.

Alexander squatted to pick up his race car. That's when he saw something that sent shivers up his spine.

An angry creature peered at him from under the ping-pong table.

Actually, it was a picture of an angry creature. Printed on a small card.

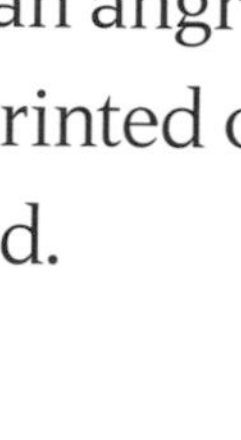

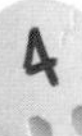

COLOSSAL FOSSIL

LEVEL 8

It's got a bone to pick with you!

ATTACKS BONE-BONK! 50 PLASTER-SPLAT! 70

HABITAT

Underground, for 200 million years.

DIET

Milk (good for growing bones)!

TYPE

THINGY

UNKNOWN

Colossal fossils come in three forms: bitter bones, furious footprints, and pesky plants.

MONSTER MEETING

The next morning, Alexander started his day at turbo speed. He hurried through breakfast, charged out the door, and raced downtown.

He parked at the library. Then he checked to make sure nobody was watching as he ducked around back into the woods.

The woods were dark. And cool. And quiet. But Alexander wasn't scared. He knew the safest place in town was in these woods: the S.S.M.P. headquarters.

Nikki sat on a slide, polishing her first-place medal. “Hey, Salamander!” she called out.

Alexander grinned. Salamander was his nickname.

Rip jogged into the clearing. He saw Nikki’s medal and groaned, “Ugh! Just because you won that toy-car race yesterday doesn’t mean you’ll win the Stermont Derby!”

“Oh yeah?!” said Nikki. “Watch me!”

They began to argue.

Alexander rolled his eyes. Rip and Nikki always argued about silly things, but they had each other's back when it came to fighting monsters. Maybe it's because they *were* monsters — good monsters.

NIKKI HUBBARD
Secretly a jampire!
• Sees in the dark.
• Avoids sunlight.
• Loves to eat red, juicy stuff like cranberries.
RIP BONKOWSKI
Secretly a knuckle-fisted punch-smasher!
• Transforms when he eats sweets — but only until the sugar runs out.

Rip always has a few ants in his pocket. When they eat sweets, they turn into helper-monsters called GI-NORM-ANTS.

"Alright you two," said Alexander. "Stop fighting — we need to clean up our headquarters."

The friends looked around. There were broken bits of junk scattered about from their last monster battle.

"My ant-buddies will take care of this!" said Rip, dropping to one knee.

TCK-TCK-TCK! He made a few tongue-clicks. Three ants climbed out of his pocket. Rip crumbled a cookie on the ground.

The ants ate the crumbs and — **BA-DINK!** — transformed into super-sized blue ants. The gi norm ants began dragging junk away from the headquarters.

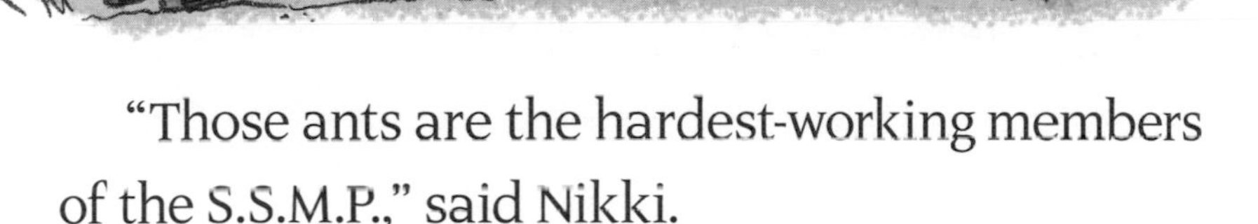

"Those ants are the hardest-working members of the S.S.M.P.," said Nikki.

"I just wish I could get them to do my homework," said Rip.

Alexander led his friends inside.

"Guess what?" he said, unzipping his backpack. "I found another monster card last night!"

He pulled out his binder.

For the past two weeks, the S.S.M.P. had been finding similar cards all over Stermont.

"It's like someone's hiding these cards just for us to find," said Nikki.

"I know!" said Alexander. "I wonder if —" He sniffed the air. "What's that horrible smell?"

CLICK-CLICK!-CLICK! A gi-norm-ant appeared in the doorway. It was carrying something on its back.

"Is that an eggshell?!" said Rip. He gave the shell a sniff. "Ugh! From a *rotten* egg! This place really *did* need a good cleaning!"

"Gross!" said Nikki.

The gi-norm-ant marched back outside, clicking happily.

"We should go," said Nikki. "Camp is about to start."

Alexander, Rip, and Nikki hurried outside.

"Wow!" said Alexander. "Your ant-buddies work fast, Rip!"

"Nice work, gi-norm-ants!" said Rip. The ants took a bow before shrinking back down and climbing into his pocket.

READY. SET. SPLAT!

Alexander, Rip, and Nikki met the rest of the campers behind the library.

"Race you to the door!" said Becka.

"You're on, weenies!" said Rip.

They all lined up at the fountain.

"Ready . . . set . . ." said May.

Something rustled in the bushes. Alexander glanced over his shoulder, but he didn't see anything.

"GO-GO-GO!" yelled Rip.

The campers sprinted toward the door.

A yellow blur roared past them.

"Oof!" Chuck fell to the ground, scraping his knee. He gave Rip an angry look. "Why did you shove me?"

"I didn't," said Rip.

"I felt a strong wind," said Becka.

"Me too," said May. "It almost knocked me over!"

Alexander gave Rip and Nikki a do-you-think-that-was-a-monster look.

"Something *definitely* flew by," whispered Nikki. "I felt it bump me!"

Then Rip stumbled. "Eww!" he said, lifting his foot. "I stepped in something stinky." His boot was dripping with slimy, stringy crud. He scraped his boot on the sidewalk.

Just then, Ms. Sprinkles opened the library door. "There you all are!" she said.

Ms. Sprinkles looked at the crud on the sidewalk. Then she squinted at the woods.

"Do you think she's looking for the monster?" whispered Rip.

"There's no way," said Alexander. "Grown-ups can't see monsters. She's probably looking for a stray dog, or whatever left that glop on the sidewalk."

Ms. Sprinkles led the campers inside. There was a checkered flag on her desk, near a display of books about race cars.

"Good morning, maker-bees!" she said. "Are you excited about the Stermont Derby?"

"Yeah!" everyone cheered.

"Me too," said Ms. Sprinkles. "I love racing! When I was a kid, I raced on the swim team."

"Awesome!" said Becka.

Ms. Sprinkles held up a silver trophy. "I won *this* in the state tournament!"

"Second place?" groaned Rip. "If you don't finish first, what's the point?"

Ms. Sprinkles winked at Rip as she placed her trophy on her desk. "A race is a game," she told the campers. "And why do we play games?"

"To win!" Rip shouted, punching the air.

Ms. Sprinkles shook her head.

"To have fun?" asked May.

"Exactly!" said Ms. Sprinkles. "And speaking of fun, today we have a surprise guest coming to talk to us about the Derby — a real race car driver!"

The campers cheered again.

"He's waiting downstairs," said Ms. Sprinkles. "I'll go get him."

As Ms. Sprinkles left the room, the campers chatted happily. Except for Nikki. She gasped.

"Rip! Salamander!" she whispered. "My medal is missing!"

MARCO SWIFT

Alexander looked Nikki up and down. "Where did your medal go?" he asked.

"Did you lose it in the woods?" asked Rip.

"I didn't *lose* it — it was stolen!" whispered Nikki. "I think that yellow-blur-thing swiped my medal when it bumped into me outside!"

"The slimy-crud-blur-thing steals medals?" said Rip.

"There must be a new monster in town!" whispered Alexander. He wrote some notes in his binder.

Ms. Sprinkles walked back into the room. "Okay, maker-bees," she said. "Please welcome professional auto racer Marco Swift!"

A tired-looking man in an apron shuffled into the room.

"*Retired* auto racer, actually," he said. "I don't race anymore. These days I run the grocery store in town — the Speedy-Mart. Here, have a snack! Only $2.49 a pound."

He gave everyone a piece of cauliflower.

Ms. Sprinkles cleared her throat. "Mr. Swift, I was hoping you could give our young racers some driving tips as they prepare to race in the Stermont Derby."

"Oh, certainly," said Mr. Swift. "Here's my tip: Skip the race!"

"Huh?" said Rip.

Mr. Swift frowned. "I used to *love* racing. But after 17 wipeouts, I realized racing is way too dangerous! That's why I wrote my own fable to share with you today: The Tortoise and the Turtle."

Mr. Swift gently set two green puppets on the table. Then he waited.

"Uh, Mr. Swift?" said Chuck. "Those puppets aren't doing anything."

"Exactly!" said Mr. Swift. "Tortoise and Turtle stayed in their shells and they never, ever raced. Sure, they didn't win a trophy. But they both lived long lives. The end."

The campers munched their cauliflower in silence.

"Uh, thanks, Mr. Swift," said Ms. Sprinkles. "Your story was . . . slow and steady."

"You think *that* was slow?" said Mr. Swift. "Wait 'til you hear my *next* fable!" He set a sloth puppet on the table. The puppet slumped over.

The campers' shoulders slumped, too.

Alexander could tell they were in for a long, slow morning.

REVVED UP

After six more slow-animal fables, lunchtime rolled around. Ms. Sprinkles led the campers to the park to eat.

As Alexander opened his lunchbox, he heard a loud noise out on the street.

VROOOOM-VROOO-VA-ROOOOOMMMM!!!

Everyone looked up.

"That car is so loud!" said Becka.

SKREEEEEE!

"Ugh! Its tires are squealing!" said May, plugging her ears.

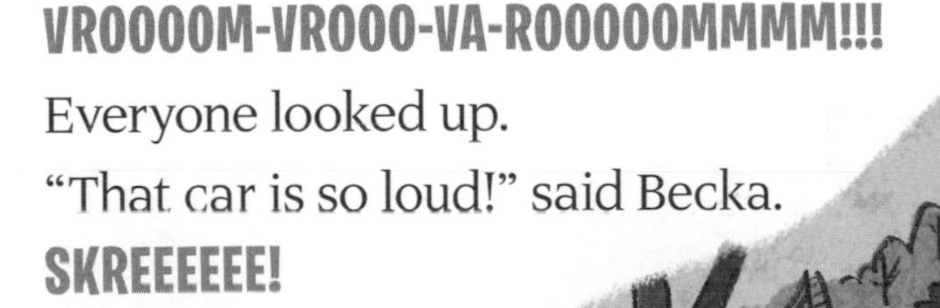

Rip laughed. "Someone's ready for the Derby!"

Ms. Sprinkles shook her head and sighed. "Why do people rev their car engines like that? It's so rude!"

Alexander peeked out from behind a tree. He didn't see a car, but he did see skid marks on the pavement, near a stop sign.

Yikes, he thought, *someone was driving way too fast!*

After lunch, Ms. Sprinkles had the campers gather around the whiteboard.

"Now comes the fun part!" she said. "It's time to design your race cars!"

THIS WEEK'S MAKER-CHALLENGE
TODAY
* Draw your car.
* Make a plan.
How will your car work?
TONIGHT
* Start building your car at home.
TOMORROW
* GAME! Plan your race strategy!
TOMORROW NIGHT
* Finish building your car at home.
SATURDAY
* RACE IN THE DERBY!

The campers got right to work. Alexander grabbed a book about race cars and plopped onto a beanbag. He spent the whole afternoon brainstorming his dream car.

Before he knew it, it was time to go.

"Everyone take your plans home tonight and start building your cars," said Ms. Sprinkles. "Tomorrow, we'll —"

VROOM-VROOOM! The engine outside roared again, loud enough to rattle the windows.

"My goodness," said Ms. Sprinkles. "That driver sounds dangerous!"

Yes, thought Alexander. *Almost as dangerous as a monster . . .*

RUINED PLANS

Alexander showed Rip and Nikki his race car plans on the walk home.

"Cool radio!" said Nikki.

"That shark fin rules!" said Rip.

"Thanks!" Alexander replied. "I'm most excited about the turbo-booster. Hopefully Dad can help me. Hey, look!" He squatted to study the sidewalk. "What are these weird tracks?"

"Skid marks," said Rip.

"Hmmm," said Alexander. "I saw some during lunch, too — near the stop sign by the park."

"These skid marks have a strange pattern," said Nikki, bending down. "See the pointy zigzag shapes?"

"Like candy corn," said Rip.

"Or fangs," said Nikki.

Alexander looked through his rolled-up plans like a telescope. "These tracks run over the curb, and straight to the Speedy-Mart," he said.

Suddenly, out of nowhere —

A yellow blur roared by. It whooshed past Alexander, spinning him in place.

"That was the same blur we saw this morning!" said Nikki.

"It's *got* to be a monster!" said Alexander.

"Uh, Salamander?" said Rip. "Look what that blur did to your race car plans!"

Alexander's heart sank. His plans had been ripped to shreds.

"This monster must have huge claws!" said Nikki.

"Maybe it's a sword-headed-chainsaw-monster!" said Rip.

"Do you think it trashed my drawing on purpose?" asked Alexander.

"I think it could've been aiming for any of us," said Nikki. "We should be careful tonight!"

The three friends rushed home to work on their cars.

Alexander's dad was in the garage, gluing sequins on fabric.

"Hiya, kiddo!" he said. "I just finished your uniform for the Derby!" He held up a white jumpsuit. "The best part is, I get to be your sponsor!"

"Uh, thanks, Dad." said Alexander. "It looks . . ."

"Groovy, I know!" said Alexander's dad. "Now, let's start building your car. What did you cook up at camp today?"

Alexander tried to explain his plans from memory. “Well, my car should have huge fins and big, comfy seats. Oh, and a radio! And a turbo-booster that can —”

Alexander’s dad laughed. “Oh, Al, those things are all too complicated. We have to build your car out of the junk in the garage!”

“Oh,” said Alexander. The shreds of his plans fell to the garage floor.

THE RED SPORTS CAR

Alexander met up with Rip and Nikki on his walk to the library the next day.

"Salamander!" said Rip. "Mom and I finished my car last night. You won't believe how fast it is!"

"Not as fast as mine!" said Nikki.

Alexander sighed. "I'm sure your cars are both faster than my tricycle-crate-sled," he said.

"Cheer up, weenie!" said Rip. "Look what I found under Mom's toolbox!"

He handed Alexander another monster card.

COW-CULATOR

LEVEL 9

An angry bull who loves math.

ATTACKS **MADDITION!** 30 **MOO-TIPLICATION!** 75

HABITAT

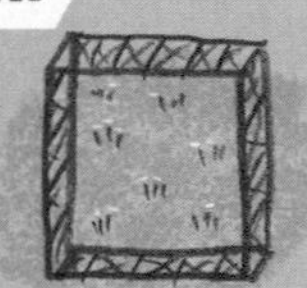

Perfectly square pastures.

DIET

3¾ bushels of corn
+ 90 C-batteries
x 365 days.

TYPE

THINGY

CRITTER

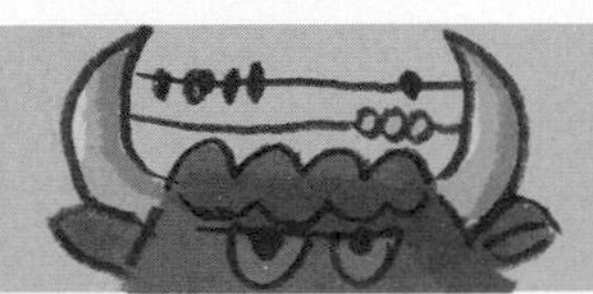

This monster has a real beef with people who don't like fractions.

Alexander tucked the card into his binder. "I wonder if the blur-monster left you this card."

Just then — **VROOOOM!** A red sports car flew down the road.

"Yikes!" said Nikki. "Why would anyone drive so fast?"

"Maybe because the speed limit is 200 miles per hour," said Rip. He pointed to a nearby sign.

"That's not right. Someone added a zero!" said Alexander.

They moved in for a closer look.

SPLATCH! Rip stepped in another pile of stringy, squishy crud.

"Not again!" Rip yelled. "Where is this stuff coming from?"

"Yuck! It's all over the signpost," said Nikki. "And look! The back of the sign is scratched up!"

"It's a message!" said Alexander. "And not a very nice one."

"Sheesh!" said Nikki. "Somebody is way too competitive!"

"They should read my latest comic!" said Rip. He handed two scribbled pages to Alexander and Nikki.

They read Rip's comic while they walked to the library.

BUCKLE UP!

RIP'S GOLD-MEDAL GUIDE TO BEING A WINNING WINNER WHO COMES IN FIRST!

The first race happened 85 million years ago, when a T. rex raced a triceratops for a burrito.

I WIN!

Dang. It's a veggie burrito.

Racing has evolved since then.

Today, there are race cars that can go more than 200 miles per hour. They could make the drive from my house to school in 9 seconds!

I could set my alarm for 7:59 and still get to school on time.

HOW TO
WIN
AT CAR
RACING:

1. Train for hours.

2. Rock cool sunglasses.

3. Learn to love speed.

Yay!

4. And most importantly, figure out how to tell left from right.

?

If you've mastered these four skills, you have what it takes to WIN!*

*Unless I'm in the race. Then you're going down, weenie!

KNOW YOUR RACING FLAGS

Can you tell which of these flags are real and which are fake?

1. GREEN FLAG: Start race.

2. YELLOW FLAG: Caution.

3. RED FLAG: Stop.

4. FLAG WITH RED AND YELLOW STRIPES: Track is slippery. Watch for oil.

5. FLAG WITH RED AND YELLOW WAVY LINES: Track is slippery. Watch for ketchup and mustard.

6. BLACK FLAG: You need to make a pit stop.

7. SPLOTCHY FLAG: You need a car wash.

18

8. GOLF FLAG: You're on the wrong course.

9. CHECKERED FLAG: Race is over.

10. CHECKERED TABLE CLOTH: Time to celebrate at a nice pizza restaurant!

ANSWER: Numbers 5, 7, 8, and 10 are not real racing flags—but they should be!

"Check it out!" said Rip. "Someone has been off-roading at the library!"

Alexander and Nikki looked up from the comic. There were tire tracks across the lawn.

"And look at all those muddy pawprints!" said Nikki.

The S.S.M.P. followed the pawprints from the ruined lawn, up the sidewalk, and into the library.

ROLL WITH IT

Alexander burst inside with Rip and Nikki at his heels. There were muddy pawprints everywhere.

Ms. Sprinkles was wiping off her desk and mumbling, "How did a dog get in here? And why did it run off with my swim trophy?"

Alexander looked at the messy counter. The checkered flag was shredded. And Ms. Sprinkles's silver cup was gone.

"There's no way a dog did this," Alexander whispered to Rip and Nikki.

"Do you think it was the blur-monster?" asked Rip.

"It had to be!" said Alexander.

"Yes," agreed Nikki. "That flag's been ripped to ribbons, just like Salamander's plans!"

The campers helped Ms. Sprinkles clean up. Then they spent the rest of the day making a giant model of the Stermont Derby race course.

"Well done, maker-bees!" said Ms. Sprinkles. "It's time for a pretend race!"

She set out a box of toy cars and a pile of dice.

The campers cheered.

"So what's the secret to winning a race?" Ms. Sprinkles asked.

"Speed!" yelled Rip.

"No, Rip," said Ms. Sprinkles. "Strategy!"

She hung up a poster listing the game rules.

DICE-n-DASH
1. Roll as many dice as you like.
2. Move your car that many spaces in a straight line.
3. Watch out for turns!
4. First car to cross the finish line wins!
1

Each camper chose a car and rolled two or three dice. They moved their cars along the track.

Then it was Rip's turn.

"Outta my way, slugs!" he said, grabbing a fistful of dice.

Everyone rolled their eyes as Rip rolled his dice.

Rip counted the spots. “Yes! Thirty-five!” He moved his car forward — straight through a corner and off the track.

“Watch that corner, speedy!” said Nikki. “You landed in the goose pond!”

“Dang,” he said, turning red. “I guess I’m out.”

The rest of the campers kept playing.

Becka, who only rolled two dice each round, crossed the finish line first.

“Nice driving, Becka!” said Ms. Sprinkles. “The key to winning is knowing when to go fast, and when to take it slow.”

Rip grumbled to Alexander and Nikki as they left the library that afternoon. “Ms. Sprinkles and Becka and Marco Swift are all wrong! I still say speed is more important than —”

The red sports car roared down the street.

“That fast car is back!” said Rip.

“Who’s driving it?” asked Alexander.

“Let’s follow it and find out!” said Nikki.

The three friends followed the car into a parking garage behind the Speedy-Mart.

“Duck down!” said Rip. “The driver’s getting out.”

“Is it the blur-monster?” asked Alexander.

“No,” said Rip. “It’s just some business dude. It looks like the real estate guy who sold Mom our house.”

They watched the man leave the garage.

"Hmmm," said Alexander. "I guess the red car has nothing to do with the monster."

"Look!" interrupted Nikki. She pointed to the garage floor. "Skid marks!"

These skid marks led to a ramp heading to the lower level of the garage. The ramp was blocked off by caution tape.

"Well, what are we waiting for?" asked Rip.

The three friends ducked under the tape and headed down.

WALKING ON EGGSHELLS

The lower level of the parking garage reminded Alexander of a dungeon.

"It's so dark down here," he said.

Nikki took a few steps forward. Her footsteps echoed off the cement walls.

"Wait up, jampire!" said Rip. "We can't see in the dark like you can."

Alexander grabbed his flashlight from his backpack and flipped it on.

A broken-down car was parked a few feet away.

"That car's been trashed," whispered Rip.

"By the blur-monster!" added Alexander.

"Check out the license plate," said Nikki. "This is Marco Swift's car!"

"The trunk is open," said Rip. "Let's peek inside."

They walked behind the car. Alexander pointed his flashlight at the trunk.

BLING! The garage glittered with light. The trunk was filled with gold, silver, and bronze trinkets.

"It's full of treasure!" Rip shouted. "We're RICH!"

"It's not treasure," said Alexander. "Those are trophies. And ribbons . . . and medals!"

"There's my medal!" said Nikki. She reclaimed hers and pinned it back onto her hoodie.

"Mr. Swift *must* be the blur-monster!" said Alexander.

"But why would he ruin his own car?" asked Rip.

VURRRR-URRR-URRRR!!! A low growl rumbled from off in the garage.

"What was that?" whispered Nikki.

Alexander turned around.

CRUNCH! Something cracked under his shoe.

"What did you step on?" asked Rip.

Alexander pointed the light at his feet.

"An egg . . ." he said. A second later, his eyes watered from a strong, foul odor. "A *rotten* egg!"

Alexander swung his light around. Hundreds of egg cartons were piled against the wall, near a mound of slimy eggshells.

VURRRR-URR-URRR . . . The growling thing rumbled closer.

"It sounds like a car is coming this way," whispered Alexander.

FWOOM! A pair of bright lights blasted the garage.

The three friends turned around.

"Ack!" said Nikki.

"Those headlights are SO bright!" yelled Rip.

Alexander shielded his eyes as the source of the light rolled closer.

Finally, he peeked over his hands. *Those aren't headlights*, he thought. *They're eyes!*

THE BLUR, IN FOCUS

VURRRR-URR-URRR-OOM!!! With a thunderous purr, the monster rolled toward the S.S.M.P.

"It's a car!" said Nikki.

"It's a cat!" said Rip.

"You're both right," growled the monster. Her white fangs glistened in the light. "I am the speedah-cheetah — the fastest monster alive. And I'm hungry!"

"Run!" Alexander yelled.

The three friends started to run. But they only made it a few steps before —

VA-ROOOOM! The cheetah peeled out and swerved in front of them.

"Whoa-whoa-whoa! Pump the brakes, kids," she said. "I'm not going to eat you. Yet."

The monster drove up closer to Alexander, Rip, and Nikki. Her tail brushed against their legs as she dragged a carton of eggs from the pile. **GLOMP!** She scarfed down a dozen eggs and — **SPLORCH!** — spat out the shells.

"Gross!" said Rip. "You eat rotten eggs?"

"Yes! Both kinds! I snack on these rotten eggs from the Speedy-Mart dumpster . . ." She crunched another egg. Goo dribbled down her chin. ". . . but my favorite kind of rotten egg is a *loser*. You know, *last one there's a rotten egg*?"

The speedah-cheetah held up a front wheel and flicked her wrist. **SHWIP!** Sharp claws sprung from the rubber.

The S.S.M.P. jumped back.

"I love playing with my food — in this case, YOU — before I eat." The speedah-cheetah took a playful swipe at Nikki with her tire.

"Let us go, eggbreath!" Rip yelled.

"Okay, sure!" said the monster. "So long as you accept my challenge."

"What challenge?" asked Alexander. He glanced at his friends.

The speedah-cheetah leaned in close. Alexander felt the monster's hot, eggy breath on his face. "I'll race you all tomorrow in the Stermont Derby," she said. "If I win, I'll eat you and all the other rotten eggs — I mean, losers!"

"What if *we* win?" asked Rip.

HUR-HUR-HUR-HAWWW! The speedah-cheetah laughed a low, rumbly laugh. "That's *highly* unlikely. But if one of you wins, I'll hightail it out of town. Now, SCAT!"

She raised up her haunches. Then she spun her wheels hard and lowered them to the garage floor. **SQUEEEEEEE!** The monster's squealing tires filled the garage with thick, white smoke.

Alexander, Rip, and Nikki coughed and sputtered.

"Let's get out of here!" yelled Alexander as they ran from the garage.

"We *have* to win that race!" said Nikki, gasping for air outside.

"There's no way!" said Rip. "How can we beat a cheetah and a race car *combined*?! Those are two of the fastest things on the planet!"

"We've got to try!" said Nikki.

"Yes," agreed Alexander. "Tonight, do whatever you can to make your cars as fast as possible. And see what you can learn about cheetahs. This monster must have a weakness!"

THE STERMONT DERBY

"Look at all these neat vehicles, Al!" said Alexander's dad the next morning.

Everyone was downtown, either getting ready to watch the race or setting up their cars at the starting line.

Alexander looked around. There were cars made from bicycles, bathtubs, bed frames, and baby buggies.

He saw a few large vehicles that looked like parade floats: a dragon, a ship, and a huge snail. But no sign of the cheetah-monster.

"I see your friends, Al!" said Alexander's dad. **BEEP-BEEP!** He honked the horn as he wheeled Alexander's race car toward Rip and Nikki.

"Hi, Dr. Bopp," said Nikki.

"Morning, Salamander. Nice outfit!" said Rip.

"Yeah!" said Nikki. "Those sequins are a good look for you!"

"See, Al? I told you your friends would like your snazzy racing suit," said Alexander's dad.

Alexander tugged at his sparkly collar. "Uh, thanks, everyone," he said.

Alexander's dad took a closer look at Alexander's friends' cars. "You two built spiffy speedsters!"

"Thanks!" said Rip. "Check out my steering wheel. It's a Frisbee!"

"And my car has a glove compartment," said Nikki.

"Neat!" said Alexander's dad. "Well, the race is about to start. Good luck, you three!" He strolled away, joining the crowd.

Nikki pointed to her glove compartment. "It's actually a lunchbox, in case I get hungry. Who else wants a strawberry gummy?"

CLACK! She flipped the latch. Alexander gasped.

A monster card fell out of her lunchbox.

"How did that get in there?!" Nikki asked. She handed the card to Alexander.

MISTY FIST

LEVEL 5

A punchy cloud of vapor.

ATTACKS DRIZZLE-CLIP! 30 FOG-WALLOP! 30

HABITAT

Broken-down lighthouses.

DIET

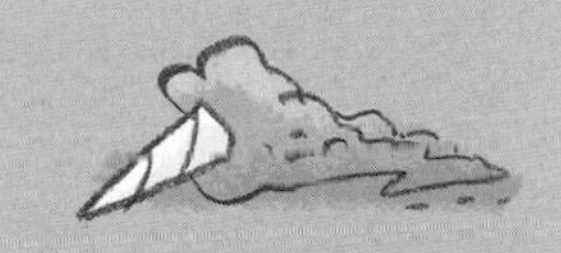

Soggy cotton candy.

TYPE

THINGY

UNKNOWN

Misty fists always pick fights on hazy days.

Alexander stuck the card in his binder. "We'll study it later," he said. "Right now, we've got a race to win!"

They wheeled their cars to the starting line, next to Becka, May, Chuck, and the giant snail float.

Alexander squeezed into his car.

"Salamander," Rip whispered. "I read up on cheetahs last night: They are fast, cunning carnivores. And their pattern allows them to blend in."

"Speaking of blending in," said Nikki, looking around, "where *is* the speedah-cheetah?"

"Maybe she didn't show. That means we would win!" said Rip. "Especially against these oversized racers! I mean — look at that snail! I *know* we'll go faster than that!"

The judge stepped up to the starting line.

"ON YOUR MARKS," he called, raising a green flag.

Alexander looked down the line. There was still no sign of the cheetah.

"GET SET!"

Just then, Alexander heard a low purring sound. **VURRR-URR-URR . . .** He tilted his head — the purr was coming from the snail float.

"GO!"

VURR-URR-ROOOOOM!! The snail took off. At cheetah speed.

THE EXPLODING SNAIL

The giant snail flew from the starting line, its shell shaking and crumbling. Suddenly —

KER-PLAM! The speedah-cheetah burst from the float! The monster rocketed down the street. Its rear wheels spun hard on the pavement, leaving behind a thick cloud of white smoke. It was impossible to see anything.

CRASH! BAM! WHAM! Alexander heard cars crashing all around him. He snapped on his goggles.

Rip waved the smoke away from his face. "A smokescreen?!" he yelled. "This monster is not playing fair!"

"That cheetah is a cheater!" said Nikki, between coughs.

As the smoke cleared, Alexander saw that most of the racers — including Becka, May, and Chuck — had piled up right at the starting line. Luckily, he and his friends were still in the race.

Nikki pedaled her car over to Alexander and Rip. "Quick!" she said. "The monster's way ahead of us already!"

RRRRRRT! The speedah-cheetah skidded to a halt halfway down the first stretch of track, leaving a long, black skid mark. Then she stood on her hind wheels and started to dance.

"You slowpokes will never catch me!" yelled the monster.

"Who's she calling 'slow'?!" said Rip. He tightened his grip on his steering wheel. "Let's roll, Monster Patrol. We've got a cat to catch."

CHEATIN' CHEETAH

SQUEAK-SQUEAK-SQUEAK! Alexander pedaled his tricycle-crate sled as hard as he could. Rip and Nikki pulled slightly ahead of him.

The speedah-cheetah waited for Alexander to catch up. Then she circled around him, baring her fangs. "Awwww . . . The little squeaker is already getting tired! I'm so happy I could cry!" She ripped a checkered flag off a lamppost and used it to blow her nose. "In just a few minutes I'll be eating your friends! And all the other losers in Stermont."

"Never!" shouted Alexander. He gritted his teeth and found a burst of energy.

Alexander, Rip, and Nikki all pedaled past the monster, who was still dancing in the street.

"Keep . . . going!" shouted Nikki, between breaths. "She's . . . overly . . . confident!"

"Huh?!" the speedah-cheetah looked up.

VROOM! She raced after the S.S.M.P. at top speed and barreled ahead, missing the turn. She slammed on the brakes, and — **POW!** — skidded into a mailbox.

Mail rained down on the dizzy monster, who was flat on her back.

Alexander stopped pedaling. "Rip! Nikki!" he shouted. "Think about it: All those skid marks we've seen around town — they were at corners. The speedah-cheetah flies off the road *at corners*!"

"It's like Dice-N-Dash!" said Rip.

"Yes!" said Nikki. "The speedah-cheetah keeps rolling a thirty-five when a seven would do the trick!"

"The speedah-cheetah might keep beating us on straightaways," said Alexander. "But if we're careful on the turns, we've got a chance of winning this race!"

"Let's move!" Rip honked his horn. **BLAAAP!**

The monster's ears perked up. She blasted off, leaving a trail of junk mail in her wake.

The three friends followed the course into Derwood Park. The road twisted, turned, and looped all through the park.

Alexander, Rip, and Nikki made headway, while behind them the monster slid around on the loose gravel.

"It's working — she's taking the curves too fast!" Rip shouted. "We're going to beat this four-wheeled fleabag! And I'll be coming in first!" Rip drifted around a corner, passing Nikki and taking the lead.

The monster pulled closer to the three friends. Her snout was within snapping distance of Alexander's rear wheel.

"You'll never beat me, kid!" she growled. She revved up her engine, and cut through the grass. Then she zoomed up a slide, using it like a ramp.

The S.S.M.P. pedaled hard as the monster sailed overhead.

"SHORTCUT!" roared the cheetah.

"Hey! Quit cheating!" yelled Nikki.

PLOMP! The speedah-cheetah landed in front of Rip. Then she twitched and made retching sounds.

YARF! She hacked up a giant, greasy hairball in the middle of the road.

"Blechh! Those are *hairballs* I've been stepping in?!" Rip yelled. He slammed on the brakes. But he was too late.

Alexander gasped as he watched Rip's car slide into the slimy hairball and flip over.

"Rip!" Nikki called. "Are you okay?"

A moment later, Rip gave a thumbs-up from beneath his car.

"See you rotten eggs at the finish line!" yelled the monster. Then she sped off, showering Rip with pebbles.

CRASH COURSE

Alexander and Nikki pulled over to the side of the course. Rip's car was totaled.

Rip climbed out of the wreck, holding his steering wheel. "I'm fine!" he said "Go on without me! You could still win!"

Alexander high-fived Rip. Then he and Nikki pedaled out of the park.

Up ahead, the speedah-cheetah struggled to stay on the track as she zig-zagged between traffic barriers.

"I see more turns ahead!" said Nikki. "Take them nice and easy, Salamander!"

Alexander and Nikki hugged the turns and soon caught up to the angry monster.

"You again?!" growled the speedah-cheetah.

Alexander pedaled with all his might. There was one last corner coming up, near the Speedy-Mart. He needed to go fast, but not *too* fast.

Alexander and Nikki zipped up next to the speedah-cheetah.

The monster slid a bit, bumping against a traffic barrier.

"She can't control her speed!" shouted Alexander. "She's going to fly off the turn!"

The speedah-cheetah's eyes grew wide as she saw the final turn coming up. Then she looked over at Alexander. "If I wipe out, I am taking you with me!"

VRRRRRR-ROWM! The monster's growl was high-pitched, like a jet engine, as she rammed into Alexander and Nikki's cars.

SPACK! The three of them hit the curb, hard. The speedah-cheetah flew snout-over-tail. Unfortunately, so did Alexander and Nikki.

GO, CART!

SPLAT! Alexander, Nikki, and the monster slammed into a display of melons.

Alexander's car and Nikki's car were now crushed together, dripping with melon juice and broken parts.

Marco Swift rushed out of the Speedy-Mart. "My melons are ruined!"

SPEEDY-
MART
5
MELONS

With a snort, the speedah-cheetah sprung back to her wheels. Or rather, three of her wheels.

Nikki smiled at the monster. "Ha!" she said. "Good luck racing on a flat tire!"

"You *wish* that would slow me down!" said the speedah-cheetah.

CLONK! She stole the front wheel from Alexander's tricycle and snapped it into place on her haunch. "That'll work!"

She hightailed it down the road.

"Now what?!" said Alexander.

"We can still win!" Rip shouted. He was running toward them, pointing at the Speedy-Mart entrance. "Remember: *Anything on wheels* can race!"

Alexander looked around to see what Rip was pointing at. "Of course!" he said, grabbing a shopping cart.

"It'll take a *monster* to beat this monster!" said Nikki. She pulled a fistful of gummies from her wrecked car. "Quick, Rip! Eat some sweets!"

"Hop in, you two," said Rip.

Alexander and Nikki climbed into the shopping cart while Rip gobbled the gummies.

RRAAWRRR! Rip transformed into the knuckle-fisted punch-smasher. He locked his horns against the cart's handles and ran.

WHOOSH! The three friends thundered down the street at turbo-speed.

"We're gaining on her!" cried Nikki.

The speedah-cheetah looked back at the S.S.M.P. and smiled. "You're too late!" she cried. "I'm only six tails away from the finish li—"

Monster-Rip grunted. He ran on his feet *and* his knuckles.

RATTLE-ATTLE-ATTLE-ZOOM! The cart sped up. Downtown Stermont flew by in a blur. They were neck-and-neck with the monster.

Monster-Rip panted. His horns started shrinking.

"Oh no, Rip! You're changing back!" shouted Alexander.

"Quick! Get in the cart!" said Nikki.

Rip tumbled into the cart, which was still whizzing along.

The speedah-cheetah made a great leap for the finish line. She was a whisker away from winning when the grocery cart squeaked past.

The S.S.M.P. won, by a nose.

VICTORY LAP

The speedah-cheetah roared. And so did the crowd! Confetti rained down as Alexander, Rip, and Nikki's grocery cart rattled to a stop in front of the judge's stand. The judge handed them a trophy and a check for $500.

The S.S.M.P. hopped out of their cart.

"Hooray!" said Alexander.

"We *beat-ah* the speedah-cheetah!" said Rip.

"And now we won't get eaten," said Nikki.

Ms. Sprinkles cheered from the crowd. "Way to go! You three handled those corners like real pros!"

"Thanks!" said Alexander.

1
WINNER!
$500
CHAMPIONS
JUDGE
BOPP

Nikki elbowed Alexander and Rip. She pointed to a nearby alley.

The speedah-cheetah gave Alexander, Rip, and Nikki a sour look. Then the monster peeled off and disappeared in a cloud of white smoke.

"Where'd she go?" asked Rip.

"I have a feeling that monster will be back to race another day," said Alexander.

"We'll be ready!" added Nikki.

The three champions smiled at their reflections in the Stermont Cup.

"So what are we going to do with the prize money?" asked Nikki.

Alexander saw Marco Swift shuffling down the sidewalk, his head low.

"We're going to pay for all those melons we splatted," said Alexander.

He ran over to Mr. Swift and handed him the check.

"Gee, thanks!" said Mr. Swift. "For a reckless racer, you're awfully kind." He gave Alexander a few bills in change and shuffled away.

"I can't believe I thought that guy could've been the monster," said Alexander.

"*I* can't believe you gave away our prize money!" said Rip. "We were rich! We could've bought a new bike! Or a dozen video games! Or — huh?" A large bit of paper fell on his head.

"It's another monster card!" said Nikki.

SPEEDAH-CHEETAH LEVEL 3

Part race car. Part cheetah. World's fastest monster.

ATTACKS BURNING RUBBER! 20 HAIRBALL-HACK! 25

HABITAT

Parking garage behind the Speedy-Mart.

DIET

Rotten eggs! (Both kinds.)

TYPE

THINGY

CRITTER

The speedah-cheetah roars down straightaways, but has trouble on turns.

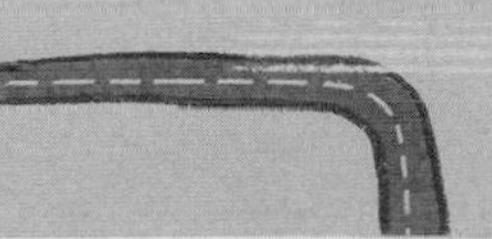

Alexander tucked the new card into his binder. Then —

"There you are!" said Alexander's dad. "Let's celebrate your victory with some ice cream!"

"Cool!" said Alexander. "It'll be my treat!"

"Race you to the ice cream shop!" said Nikki. "Last one there is a rotten egg!"

Rip, Nikki, and Alexander's dad all ran down the sidewalk. But not Alexander. He was happy to take his time.

ABOUT THE AUTHOR

NEW YORK TIMES BESTSELLING AUTHOR
TROY CUMMINGS
LEVEL 0
won a world championship car race! (In a video game.)
ATTACKS
SUPER-FAST SKETCH! 95
SLOWER ERASE! 5
HABITAT
A quiet house with loud cats.
DIET
Cheetah Omelette: Two eggs, covered with sharp, shredded cheddar and spotted with TONS of black pepper.
© H.S. INDUSTRIES

Troy Cummings has no tail, no wings, no fangs, no claws, and only one head. As a kid, he believed that monsters might really exist. Today, he's sure of it.

Mr. Cummings came up with the idea for SPEEDAH-CHEETAH when he was racing his kids through the house and stepped on a huge hairball his cats left at the finish line.

Mr. Cummings has written and/or illustrated more than thirty books, including THE NOTEBOOK OF DOOM series.

THE BINDER OF DOOM

SPEEDAH-CHEETAH

QUESTIONS & ACTIVITIES

A fable is a short story with a moral or lesson. Marco Swift tells the campers a fable he created called "The Tortoise and the Turtle." What lesson does his fable teach? Does Marco Swift's fable remind you of a famous fable? (Hint! It also stars a tortoise.)

The S.S.M.P. finds a trashed car in the parking garage. How do they know the monster destroyed this car? List three clues they find. Where have they seen similar clues before?

What do you notice about this list from page 55: "bicycles, bathtubs, bed frames, and baby buggies"? Each word starts with the same letter! This is called **alliteration**. Can you write an alliterative list, too?

The S.S.M.P. accidentally destroys Marco Swift's melon display. How do they make it up to him later? Look back at page 87.

At maker-camp, Alexander designs the race car of his dreams. What would your dream race car look like? How would you make it? Draw a picture of your race car and list the materials you would need to build it.